DRAWING WITH 4D

DRAWING ALIENS, SPACECRAFT, AND OTHER STUFF BEYOND THE GALAXY

An Augmented Reading Drawing Experience

BY CLARA CELLA

ILLUSTRATED BY S. ALTMANN

CAPSTONE PRESS

a capstone imprint

Dabble Lab Books are published by Capstone Press,
1710 Roe Crest Drive, North Mankato, Minnesota 56003
www.mycapstone.com

Library of Congress Cataloging-in-Publication data is available on the Library of Congress website.
ISBN: 978-1-5435-3187-9 (library binding)
ISBN: 978-1-5435-4236-3 (eBook PDF)
Summary: This book delivers aliens, rockets, and other out-of-this-world drawing projects with step-by-step instructions and special 4D support. Projects increase in difficulty from the first to the last to strengthen drawing skills and confidence. Readers can download the Capstone 4D app for an augmented reality experience that extends learning beyond the printed page with artist video tutorials and other bonus content.

Editorial Credits
Jill Kalz, editor; Aruna Rangarajan, designer;
Kathy McColley, production specialist

Photo Credits
Capstone Studio: Karon Dubke, 31 (zipper pulls); Shutterstock: Andrii Tokarchuk (star background), cover and throughout, Jamen Percy, 5 (pencils and scribbles), Lifestyle Graphic (sheet of paper), cover and throughout, Mega Pixel, 5 (erasers and pencil sharpener), Ruslan Ivantsov, 5 (graphite pencil), timquo, 5 (felt marker)

Printed and bound in the USA
PA017

TABLE OF CONTENTS

Download the Capstone 4D app!

- Ask an adult to download the Capstone 4D app.
- Scan the cover and stars inside the book for additional content.

When you scan a spread, you'll find fun extra stuff to go with this book! You can also find these things on the web at www.capstone4D.com using the password: alien.31879

HELLO, ARTIST!

Greetings from Planet Ooloc . . . the Pluponian Nebula . . . and the Blixby Galaxy! The 10 creatures and alien vehicles in this book have traveled a great distance to be here. Not to eat you or take you prisoner (don't worry!), but to meet you and ask you to draw their portraits.

The projects are ordered from easy to more challenging. Follow the step-by-step instructions and practice, practice, practice. Scan the star targets if your drawing starts veering off course. Your 4D instructor will help you get back on track. Before you know it, you'll have countless pages of

OUT-OF-THIS-WORLD AWESOME!

TOOLS AND SUPPLIES

Before you begin your drawing projects, gather the following tools and supplies:

PAPER

Any type of blank, unlined paper will do.

PENCILS

Pencils are the easiest to use. Make sure you have plenty of them.

SHARPENER

You'll need clean lines, so keep a pencil sharpener close by.

ERASER

Pencil erasers wear out very quickly. Get a rubber or kneaded eraser.

DARK PEN/MARKER

When your drawing is finished, you can trace over it with a black ink pen or a thin felt-tip marker. The dark lines will really make your work pop.

COLORED PENCILS

If you decide to color your drawings, colored pencils usually work best.

Qu24 Rocket

Got a large payload to haul? Then get yourself a Qu24 rocket! This rocket can lift more than 150,000 pounds (68 metric tons) of cargo into orbit. Used mostly by the kind-hearted Skrawk people, the rocket often carries food and supplies to nearby planets in need.

STEP 1

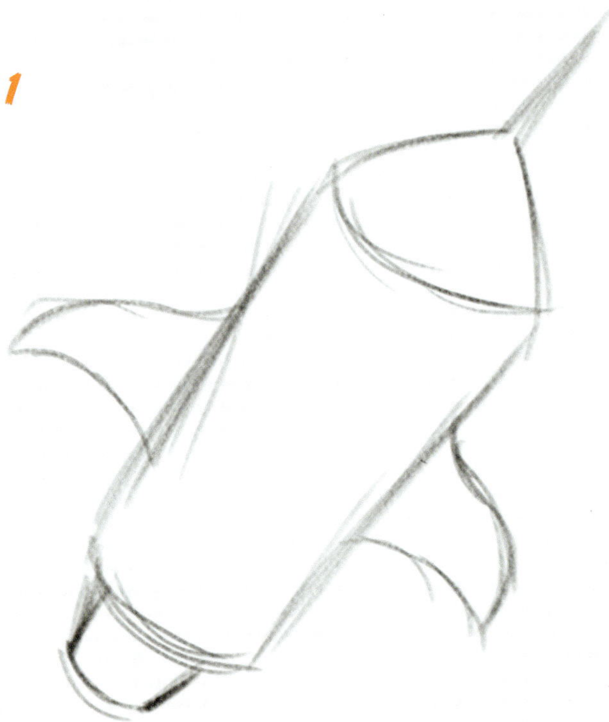

STEP 2

STEP 3

STEP 4

Try drawing a launch pad for your rocket. Include lots of smoke clouds around the base.

STEP 5

TENTACALLUS

Part frog, part octopus, and part who-knows-what. That's Tentacallus, a rarely seen underwater alien. Gentle-natured and shy, Tentacallus makes its home in the oceans of Planet Aquas. There it feasts on sea bugs and schools of tiny fish.

STEP 1

STEP 2

STEP 3

STEP 4

Draw some sea bugs and fish for Tentacallus to munch on.

STEP 5

UFO

Something zips around in the air. It hovers in place. It blinks. What is it? It's a UFO—an unidentified flying object. One of the most famous UFO sightings happened in 1947, in Roswell, New Mexico. A rancher found pieces of what he thought was an alien spaceship on his land.

STEP 1

STEP 2

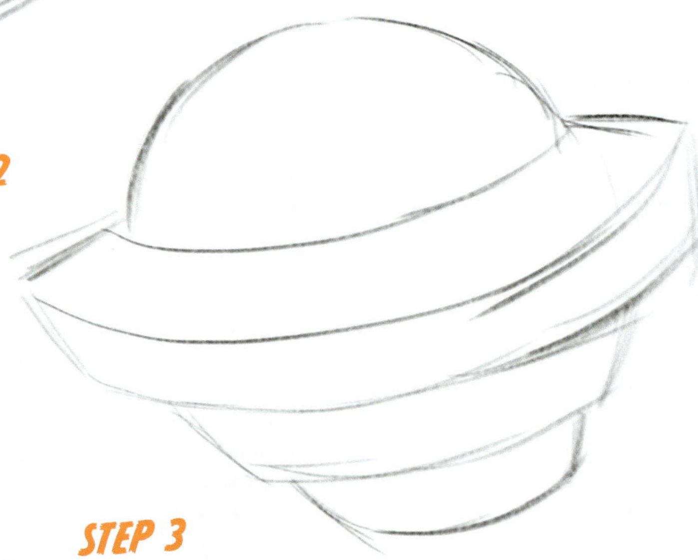

STEP 3

STEP 4

Once you've finished your UFO, draw the alien it belongs to. Is it friendly? Dangerous? Animal-like?

STEP 5

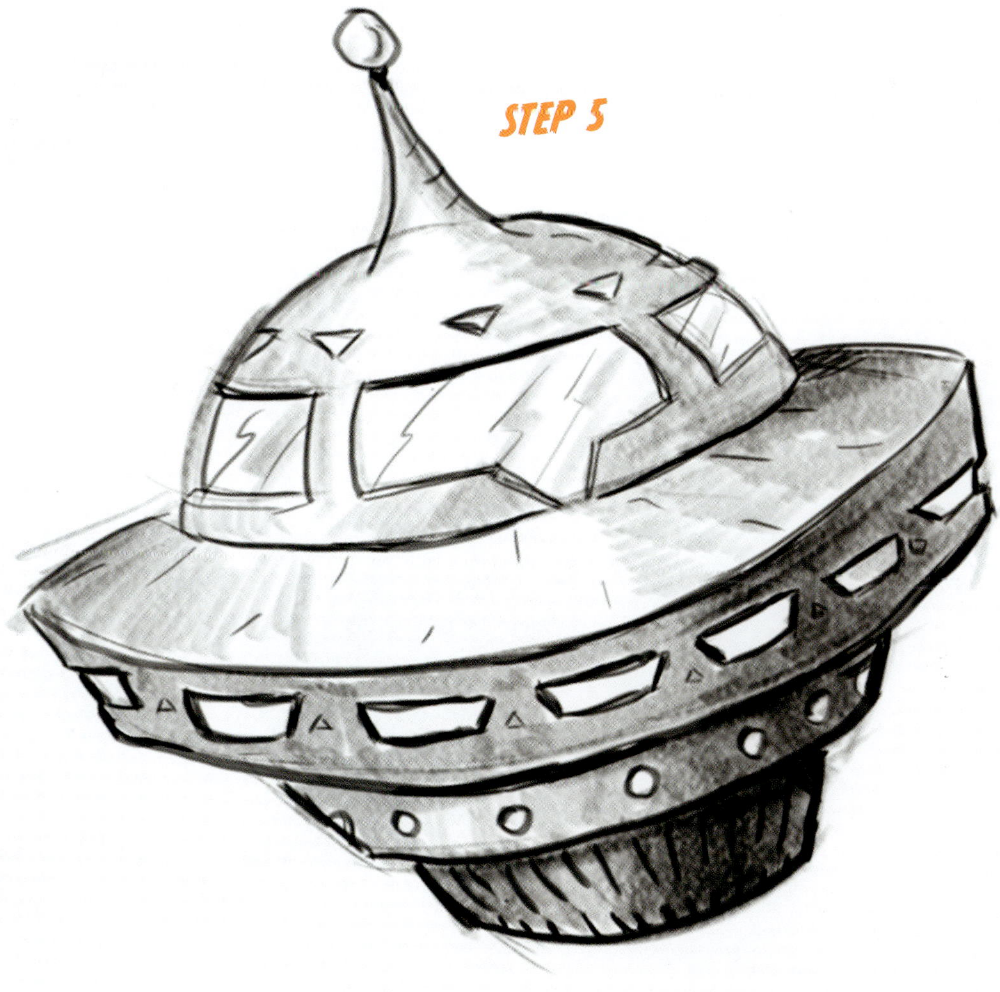

SPACE CAR

In some ways, aliens aren't much different than people. When they need to get somewhere fast, they hop in their car, just like we do. But the cool things about space cars? They fly. And they're powered by jet engines that move them faster than the speed of sound. *ZOOM!*

STEP 1

STEP 2

STEP 3

STEP 4

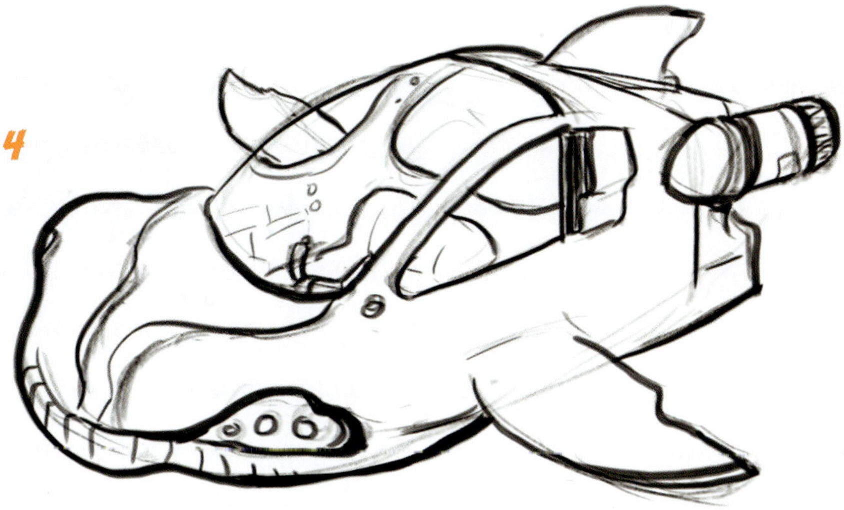

STEP 5

Draw your space car zipping around a bunch of planets and moons. Watch out for space rocks!

MADMIAN

The Madmians are tiny, tough aliens who live in the treetops of Planet Ooloc. What Madmians lack in size, they make up for in grit. They've got moves like monkeys and attack skills like great white sharks—with some weird alien stuff thrown in too.

STEP 1

STEP 2

STEP 3

STEP 4

STEP 5

Try drawing a community of Madmians swinging and leaping through an Oolocian forest.

Creature Mover

On Earth, we call this a people mover. But in outer space, it's a creature mover. Like driverless shuttles or light-rail trains, creature movers take large groups of aliens from point A to point B. Some fly in any direction, like space cars. Others float above magnetic tracks.

STEP 1

STEP 2

STEP 3

Once your creature mover is finished, draw a line of aliens, of all kinds, waiting to board.

STEP 4

STEP 5

XACTONON

A word of advice: Don't mess with a Xactonon (ZAK-toh-non)! With their razor-sharp claws and snapping jaws, Xactonons are one of the most feared aliens in any galaxy. They move fast and can leap straight up into the air. One blow from a Xactonon's fighting blade, and it's lights out!

STEP 1

Xactonons live in rocky, desert areas. Draw a home for your Xactonon (and don't forget the cacti!).

STEP 2

STEP 3

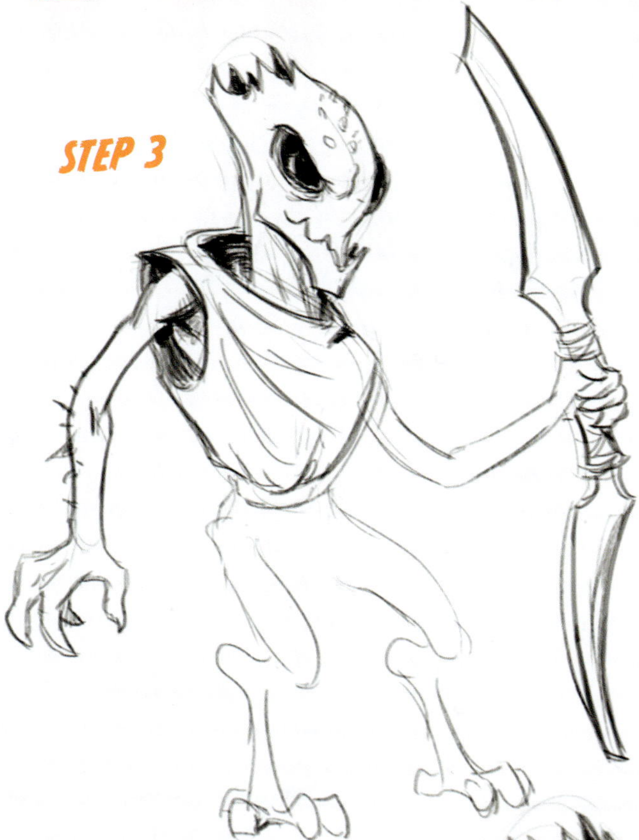

STEP 4

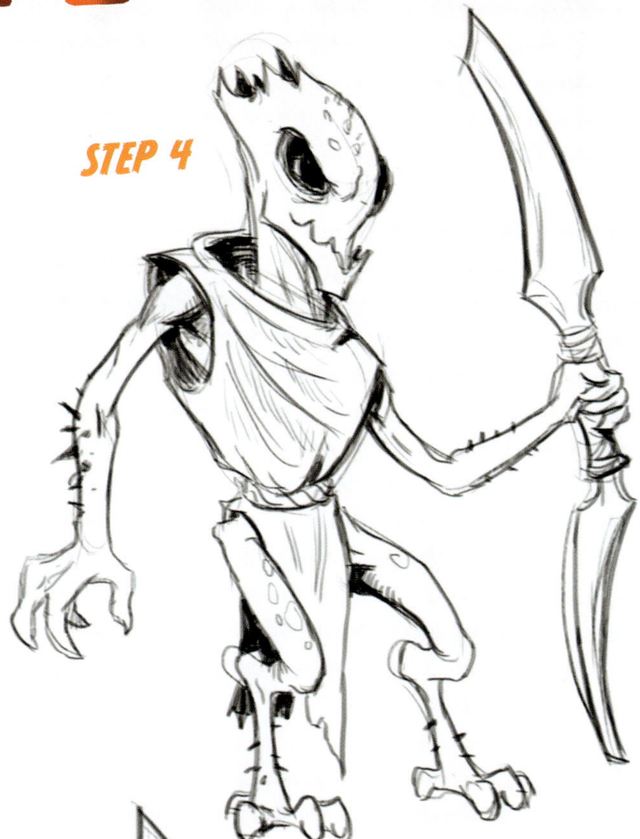

STEP 5

Repzid

No alien is cooler than a Repzid. Truth! From its goggle glasses to its long alligator tail, its trendy clothes to its jelly zapper (yep, it shoots strawberry jelly!). Repzids are fun-loving creatures and some of the most loyal alien friends you'll ever have.

STEP 1

STEP 2

STEP 3

Try drawing a funky hat on your Repzid. How about a pair of cowboy boots or high-tops?

STEP 4

STEP 5

SPACE STATION

Madmians use this space station to study plant growth in space. Decades of hot, dry weather on the Madmians' home planet, Ooloc, have nearly wiped out the food supply. The work being done in the space station is key to the Madmians' survival.

STEP 1

STEP 2

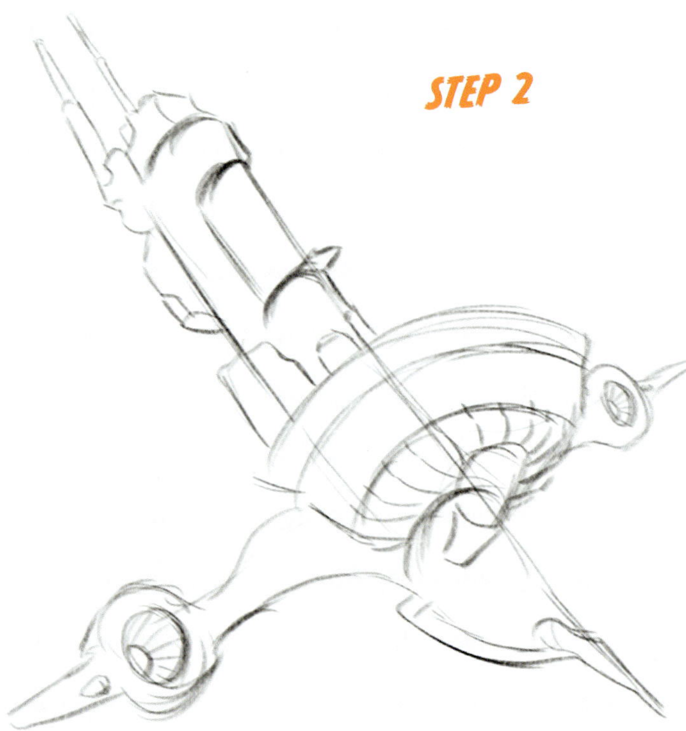

STEP 3

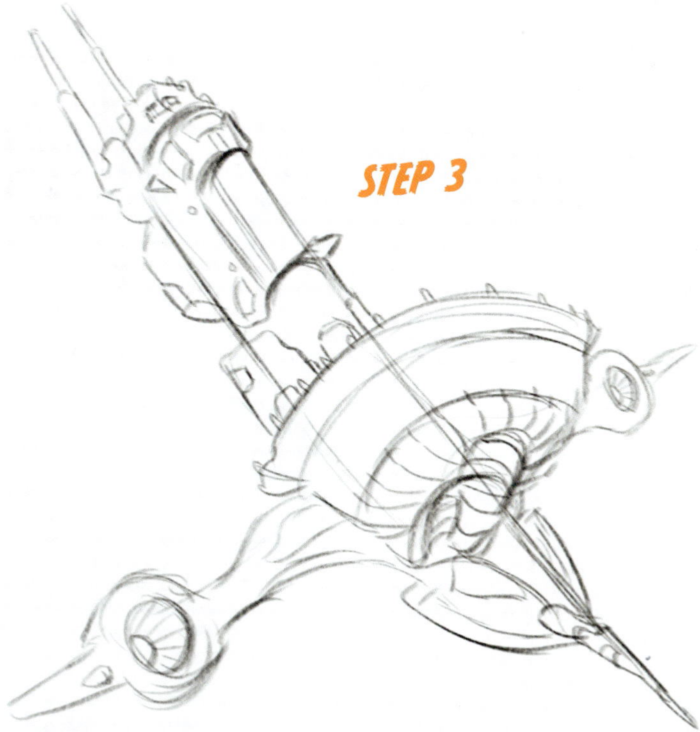

STEP 4

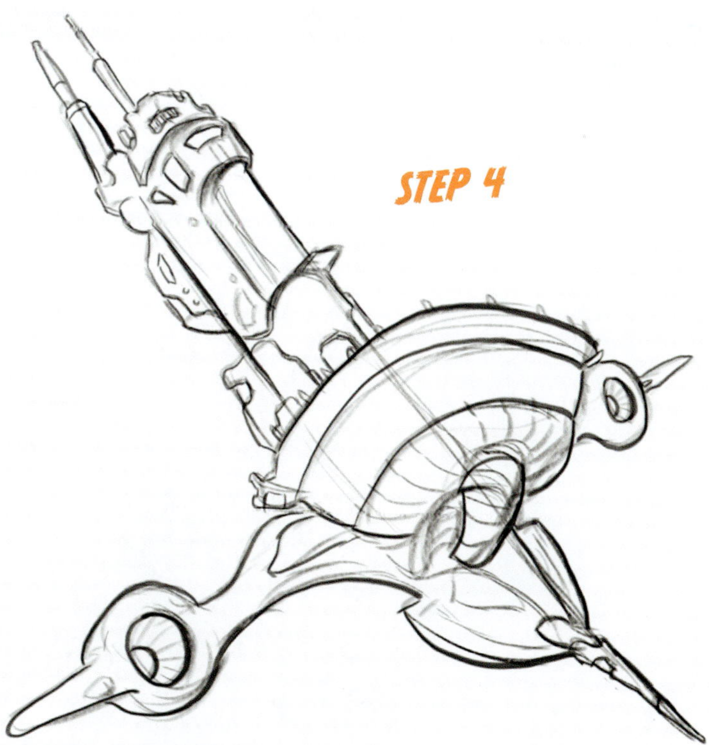

CONTINUED...

SPACE STATION CONTINUED

STEP 5

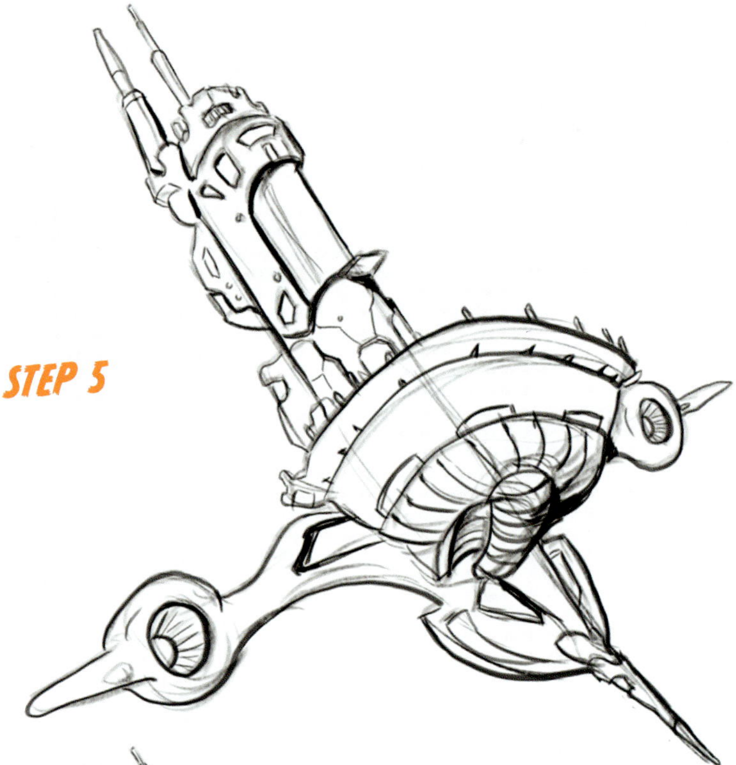

STEP 6

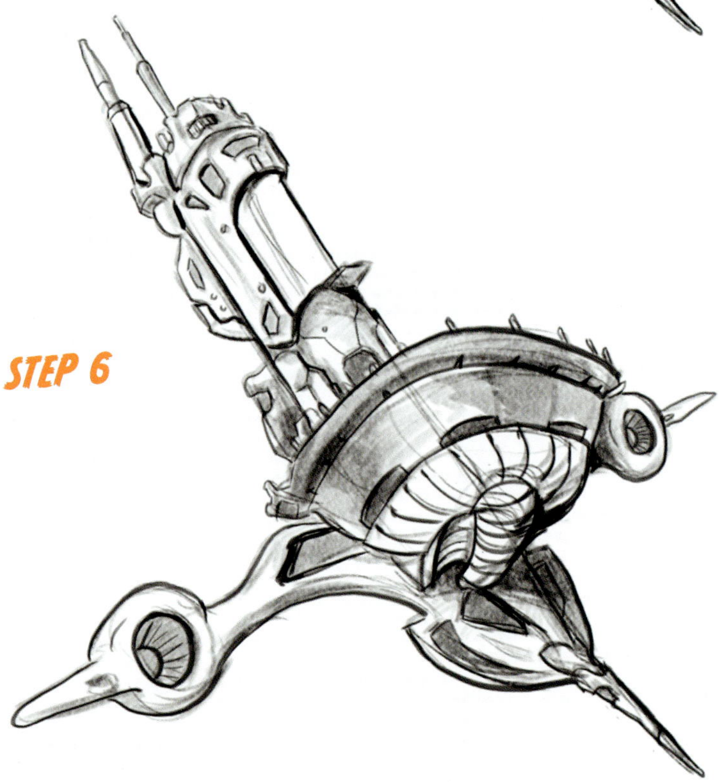

After you've drawn the space station from the outside, sketch the view from the inside.

STEP 7

Shahlahz, the Bionic Girl

Long ago, a bad accident severely injured a Florida girl named Shayla Glueck. Doctors rebuilt much of her body with mechanical parts and trained her to fight crime. With her super-strong arms, lightning-fast legs, and X-ray vision, Shayla is now known as Shahlahz, the Bionic Girl.

STEP 1

STEP 2

STEP 3

STEP 4

CONTINUED...

Shahlahz, the Bionic Girl continued

STEP 5

STEP 6

STEP 7

Show off Shahlahz's strength by drawing her smashing through a wall or lifting a bus over her head.

CRAFT IT UP!

WAY TO GO! You've turned a stack of blank paper into your own little universe. Now, let's take one of your drawings and do something with it. Craft it up!

ALIEN ZIPPER PULL

WHAT YOU NEED:

- a drawing of your favorite alien*
- shrinkable plastic sheets
- a black marker
- colored pencils
- a hole punch
- scissors
- an adult
- an oven
- a jump ring
- a lanyard hook clasp
- a key ring

STEP 1 Trace the alien onto a plastic sheet with the marker and color it with colored pencils.

STEP 2 Punch a hole where you would like to insert the jump ring.

STEP 3 Carefully cut around the image.

** Make sure the image is three to four times bigger than you want the finished product to be.*

STEP 4 With an adult's help, carefully follow the baking and cooling instructions on the shrinkable plastic sheet package.

STEP 5 Insert the jump ring into the hole. Connect the jump ring to the lanyard clasp and key ring, then hook it to your zipper. Done!

Earthling! Attach us to your zippers!

Read More

Ames, Lee J. *Draw 50 Outer Space: The Step-by-Step Way to Draw Astronauts, Rockets, Space Stations, Planets, Meteors, Comets, Asteroids, and More.* California: Watson-Guptill, 2017.

Gowen, Fiona. *How to Draw Scary Monsters and Other Mythical Creatures.* How to Draw. Hauppauge, N.Y.: Barrons Educational Series, Inc., 2017.

Hart, Christopher. *Drawing Cartoons from Numbers: Create Fun Characters from 1 to 1001. Drawing Shape by Shape Series.* New York: Drawing with Christopher Hart, 2018.

Internet Sites

Use FactHound to find Internet sites related to this book:

Visit *www.facthound.com*

Just type in 9781543531879 and go.

Makerspace Tips

Download tips and tricks for using this book and others in a library makerspace.

Visit *www.capstonepub.com/dabblelabresources*